Who Played~And How!

The official ball, the only ball ever used, was a small hard pir rubber ball that would really fly if you could catch the edge c the step. . . . It was known without fail as a "Spal-deen," with t last syllable hit as hard as possible. . . . The special pronunciatic made it our ball.

Sandy Koufax, Hall of Fame Pitcher

I slept with my Spaldeen and named it (and all of its descendants) Heathcliff. My pink ball made me very popular on the playground. I never ran out of rhymes or variations on games with a Spaldeen.

Judith Rovenger, Librarian

I loved the feel of a powdery new Spaldeen, and I never wanted to get it dirty. In my neighborhood I was often the one who had the ball. But when it landed on the grouchy old man's stoop next door, everyone was afraid to get it. Including me!

Sheldon Fogelman, Lawyer

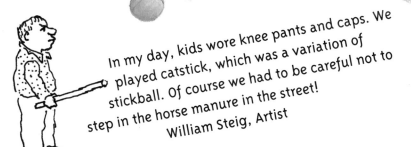

In my day, kids wore knee pants and caps. We played catstick, which was a variation of stickball. Of course we had to be careful not to step in the horse manure in the street!

William Steig, Artist

Whenever any ball came toward me—
I ducked!
Shari Lewis, Television Star

I'd play ball all day if I could.
Samantha Kantor, Age 8

Who could forget their bubble-gum pink color, intoxicating rubbery smell, and velvety-smooth surface. Perfect for writing on with a ballpoint pen!
Doris Indyke, Newspaper Reporter

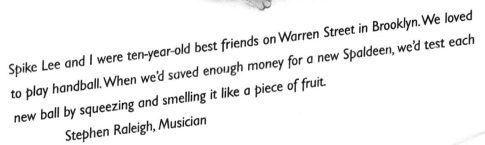

Spike Lee and I were ten-year-old best friends on Warren Street in Brooklyn. We loved to play handball. When we'd saved enough money for a new Spaldeen, we'd test each new ball by squeezing and smelling it like a piece of fruit.
Stephen Raleigh, Musician

We chose sides, and each player would take turns flinging the rubber ball against the steps while the opposing players fielded. . . . When our mothers called out from our windows, we often pleadingly responded, "Just one more lick, Mom!"
Joe Wlody, Reading Tutor

My best memories of growing up in Brooklyn all involve a Spaldeen: stickball, stoopball, points, running bases, and slap ball. When I hit the ball I felt like Mickey Mantle!
Kevin Martin, President, Spalding Sports Worldwide

Foreword

Hit-the-penny, boxball, handball, stickball, stoopball, punchball . . . the possibilities were endless. Everyone played: in the street, on the sidewalk, in schoolyards, alleyways, and abandoned lots. Playing ball was one of the privileges of living in the city.

What made all these games possible was a little pink ball. Most people called it a Spaldeen. Some called it a Pinkie. The ball made the sweetest sound—off your fist, off a mop handle or broomstick, or off the wall. It felt as fuzzy as a peach, and it smelled great, too.

Like Annie's Sky-High Super Pinkie, this legendary pink ball lives on today. In cities across the country, young and old gather for pickup games of handball or stickball. There's even a World Series championship where teams like the Bronx Old Timers and the Brooklyn Knights are apt to be found, along with a crowd of diehard fans—ready, like Annie's neighbors, for a great show.

Wait for me. I just have to put on my sneakers!

Cari Best

Last Licks

A Spaldeen Story

by
Cari Best

pictures by
Diane Palmisciano

A DK INK BOOK
DK PUBLISHING, INC.

One day during spelling, Annie Ellis itched to pitch her lucky Sky-High Super Pinkie at the blackboard behind Miss Hatchett's back.

"Be careful," whispered Spit, who understood Annie's itch.

"Not yet," warned Jay-Jay, who had the best view.

"I dare you," chided Chickie, who hoped Miss Hatchett would catch Annie in the act.

She did.

That afternoon Miss Hatchett sent a note home to Annie's family.

~PS 206~

Dear Mr. and Mrs. Ellis and Aunt Pearl,

Annie would rather play ball than spell a-u-r-o-r-a b-o-r-e-a-l-i-s.

Yours truly,
Helen Hatchett

P.S. Next time I will POP the pesky Pinkie.

"That was close," said Spit later on the bus.

"Boy, were you lucky," said Jay-Jay.

"You got a note," sang Chickie, really loud in Annie's ear.

But Annie was so happy Miss Hatchett hadn't popped her Pinkie that she forgot to worry.

"I've almost lost this ball a million times," she told Spit on the way home. "Down the sewer, on the roof, in the hedges, under a car—"

"And don't forget Mrs. O'Donnell's dog," Spit reminded her.

"But I always manage to get it back," Annie said proudly. "It's my lucky ball, and I'm going to keep it forever."

"Not if the Super gets it, you won't," said Chickie, pointing at his window.

Everyone knew about the Super's collection of Sky-High Super Pinkies. If a ball hit his window, he'd be out in a flash to claim it for his collection.

"A rule's a rule," he'd say, admiring his latest prize.

"The Super will never get my ball," said Annie, pushing her Pinkie into the deepest part of her pocket. Then she took the long way home. She was in no hurry to deliver Miss Hatchett's note to her family.

Aunt Pearl was first.
"What's with the b-a-l-l?"
she asked. "We've always been a
family of knitters, not to mention spellers."
"Knitters are sitters," said Annie. "And I'm
not good at sitting."
Her father was next. "After all is said and done,
e-n-t-o-m-o-l-o-g-y is the one. The study of
insects—what could be more exciting than
catching flies!" he said.
"The only fly I'd like to catch is a fly ball," said Annie.
Her mother was last. "If your ball doesn't roll down the sewer, it lands on the
roof. If it doesn't bounce into traffic, it gets stuck in someone's hedges. Why
don't you e-x-e-r-c-i-s-e with me?" she asked.

"Because playing ball is what *I* do," Annie answered, squeezing her Pinkie to see how much air was inside. She ran her thumb back and forth over the soft, fuzzy rubber, sniffed it, and said, "This ball is perfect for everything: punching and catching, throwing and smelling."

aurora borealis

And just to show that good ballplayers could also be good spellers, Annie wrote a-u-r-o-r-a b-o-r-e-a-l-i-s on her ball in big blue letters. "So there," she said, smiling.

Then, without wasting another second, she went
outside to play.

Over the telephone wires and off the stoops, against
the brick walls and in the squares on the sidewalks,
Annie's ball bounced like nobody's business.

NO Ball Playing Or Else!

S. PAUL DEAN
Superintendent

She punched it and slapped it,
jumped over it and clapped it,
and made sure to catch it every time.
    "My lucky ball is the best!" she
shouted as she hurried past the
Super's window.

And that night, before she went to sleep, Annie put
her one and only Sky-High Super Pinkie in her
pocket—safe from the sewers and the roofs, the traffic
and the hedges, and far away from Miss Hatchett
and the Super.

Annie could hardly wait till Sunday, her
favorite day of the week—the day when the
Super went to New Jersey to visit his sister.
The day when it was finally safe to play
punchball. Annie bounced her ball while she
brushed her teeth. "No Super today!" she
exclaimed. Then she played handball down
the hall until all the walls and ceilings were
dotted with Sky-High Super Pinkie circles.

"I'm tired of painting over the spots," said her father.
"The bouncing is giving me a headache," said Aunt Pearl.
"One of these days you're going to lose that ball," said her mother.
"Never," said Annie. "I'm never going to let it out of my sight."

When Annie got to the punchball field, the kids were already choosing up sides. Her fingers started itching, and so did her toes. Her knees started tingling, and so did her nose.

"Who's got a ball?" Chickie asked.

"The Super got mine on Friday," said Frog.

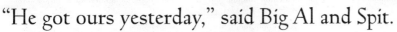

"He got ours yesterday," said Big Al and Spit.

"Annie's is the only one left," announced Jay-Jay.

The Super's in New Jersey, thought Annie. That's pretty far away. "Okay," she said, pulling her lucky Pinkie from her pocket. "Let's play!"

Spit's team was up first. Then Annie's.
There were hard hits, high pops, and little cheapies
that trickled a short way down the field.

There were

amazing catches,

close calls,

and balls that slipped through butterfingers.

Neighbors leaned out their windows to watch.

Others stopped working on their cars or crossword puzzles, or looked up from their knitting or their Sunday papers.

Gordie argued, Joe cheated, Chickie teased, and Big Al complained. Just like they did every Sunday. Everyone was having a great time.

Annie dived,

Annie leaped,

Annie stretched,

and Annie fired.

But just as she stepped up to take her turn,
everyone's mother started calling for supper:
"Al, Jay-Jay, Spit, Annie, Joe, Gordie,
Chickie, Frog, Wrench!"

"Hey," she cried. "You can't
leave! I have to get my last licks.
You guys were up first." She
shifted her shoulders. She wiggled
her legs. She squeezed the ball, blew on her
knuckles, and swung her punching
arm back and forth to warm it up.

At last she was ready. And so was the ball sitting in her hand. Ready as a rocket. She forgot about the sewers. She forgot about the roofs, the hedges, and Miss Hatchett. No ceilings to get spots on. No Super's window to worry about. It's only me and the big blue sky, Annie thought.

POP! Annie's Sky-High Super Pinkie shot into the air. Higher and higher . . . farther and farther . . . over the outfielder's heads—and Mrs. O'Donnell's, too. Over the tops of the sycamore trees, the parked cars, and the playground. Through the light and the dark and the dusk of day.

"What was that?" shouted Annie's father, dropping a spider.

"Yikes!" yelled Aunt Pearl, skipping a stitch.

"That's Annie's Pinkie!" cried her mother, sitting up and pointing.

But the ball kept going . . . and going . . . and going. Over the line of Aunt Pearl's underwear. Over Mr. Lipsky's seltzer truck, and over the Super's window. Through the dust and the wind and the "ooohs" of the crowd. Everyone started running to see where the ball would land.

Suddenly, in a frenzied flash, a familiar figure
came flying out of nowhere.

It went backward and
it went forward.

It sidestepped and
it spun around.

Finally, in a spectacular, over-the-shoulder,
one-of-a-kind, super-duper catch, it snagged
Annie's sky-high punch — with one hand.

Annie caught up with the catch—and the Super—who was just back from New Jersey.

"What a punch!" was all he could say.

"What a catch!" was all she could say.

Then, in the middle of the clapping and the shouting and the hubbub of the neighborhood, the Super said, "A rule's a rule. This ball never hit my window, so you deserve to have it back."

As Annie watched, he slowly rubbed his thumb over the soft, fuzzy rubber. He brought the Pinkie up to his nose and smelled . . . and smiled. Annie had never seen him smile before. She thought about his catch—the most spectacular catch ever. Then she let out a big sigh and said, "I think you should have my lucky Pinkie for your collection—it's the only one you're missing."

That night, for the first time, Annie's pajama pocket was empty. No lucky Pinkie to hold or to squeeze or to smell. Only the memory of the POP of the punch. And of course that super catch. Annie wondered how she'd replace the best ball she'd ever had.

The next morning, when a package arrived, she found out. Inside was a note . . .

. . . and a brand-new
Sky-High Super Pinkie.

Congratulations, Aurora Borealis!
You sure know how to play ball.
Thank you for the last (and best) addition to my collection.

Sincerely,
S. Paul Dean, Super
Sycamore Gardens

P.S. I thought you should have the enclosed.

Later that day, Annie walked by the Super's window just to get a look at her old ball. "You were great," she whispered to the Pinkie.

Her brand-new Sky-High Super Pinkie felt a little too fuzzy, bounced a little too high, and smelled a little too new. But before long, Annie knew she would get it feeling and bouncing and smelling just like her old lucky ball.

Now the neighbors pass by the Super's window just to sneak a peek, too. Aunt Pearl tells everyone, "My niece is a peach of a puncher, isn't she?" Annie's mother has found that playing ball is good exercise, and her father conducts guided tours of the Pinkie spots in their apartment. Not to mention Miss Hatchett, who is especially grateful to Annie for helping everyone in Sycamore Gardens learn to spell a-u-r-o-r-a b-o-r-e-a-l-i-s.

TOUR at 2:00

GUIDE

As for the Super, he now visits his sister on
Saturday just so he won't miss a game.

For Paulie, my best ball buddy
And for Seimi and Bob, who loved to watch us play —CB

With special thanks to Jane, Melanie, and Chris —DP

A Melanie Kroupa Book

DK Publishing, Inc.
95 Madison Avenue
New York, New York 10016

Visit us on the World Wide Web at http://www.dk.com

Library of Congress Cataloging-in-Publication Data
Best, Cari.
    Last licks / by Cari Best ; illustrations by Diane Palmisciano. — 1st ed.
        p.   cm.
    "A Melanie Kroupa book"
    Summary: Annie's spectacular hit and the ball collector's amazing catch of her Sky-High Super Pinkie
bring the two former foes together in an unexpected way
    ISBN 0-7894-2513-0
    [1. Punchball—Fiction.] I. Palmisciano, Diane, ill. II. Title.
PZ7.B46575Las 1998   97-43606
[E]—DC21   CIP
                                                                                            AC

Book design by Chris Hammill Paul.
The text of this book is set in 18 point Truesdell.
The illustrations for this book were done in oil pastel.

Printed and bound in U.S.A.

First Edition, 1999

2   4   6   8   10   9   7   5   3   1

The official ball, the only ball ever used, was a small hard p rubber ball that would really fly if you could catch the edge the step. . . . It was known without fail as a "Spal-deen," with last syllable hit as hard as possible. . . . The special pronunciat made it our ball.

Sandy Koufax, Hall of Fame Pitcher

I slept with my Spaldeen and named it (and all of its descendants) Heathcliff. My pink ball made me very popular on the playground. I never ran out of rhymes or variations on games with a Spaldeen.

Judith Rovenger, Librarian

I loved the feel of a powdery new Spaldeen, and I never wanted to get it dirty. In my neighborhood I was often the one who had the ball. But when it landed on the grouchy old man's stoop next door, everyone was afraid to get it. Including me!

Sheldon Fogelman, Lawyer

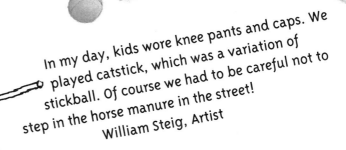

In my day, kids wore knee pants and caps. We played catstick, which was a variation of stickball. Of course we had to be careful not to step in the horse manure in the street!

William Steig, Artist

Whenever any ball came toward me—
I ducked!
Shari Lewis, Television Star

I'd play ball all day if I could.
Samantha Kantor, Age 8

Who could forget their bubble-gum pink color, intoxicating rubbery smell, and velvety-smooth surface. Perfect for writing on with a ballpoint pen!
Doris Indyke, Newspaper Reporter

Spike Lee and I were ten-year-old best friends on Warren Street in Brooklyn. We loved to play handball. When we'd saved enough money for a new Spaldeen, we'd test each new ball by squeezing and smelling it like a piece of fruit.
Stephen Raleigh, Musician

We chose sides, and each player would take turns flinging the rubber ball against the steps while the opposing players fielded. . . . When our mothers called out from our windows, we often pleadingly responded, "Just one more lick, Mom!"
Joe Wlody, Reading Tutor

My best memories of growing up in Brooklyn all involve a Spaldeen: stickball, stoopball, points, running bases, and slap ball. When I hit the ball I felt like Mickey Mantle!
Kevin Martin, President, Spalding Sports Worldwide